Book T

THE

KLONDIKE KID

Trilogy

Adventure in Gold Town

Other Ready-For-Chapters books by
Deborah Hopkinson

Book Three of

Trilogy

Adventure in Gold Town

By Deborah Hopkinson

Illustrated by Bill Farnsworth

ALADDIN PAPERBACKS
NEW YORK LONDON TORONTO SYDNEY

First Aladdin Paperbacks edition November 2004

Text copyright © 2004 by Deborah Hopkinson
Illustrations copyright © 2004 by Bill Farnsworth

ALADDIN PAPERBACKS
An imprint of Simon & Schuster
Children's Publishing Division
1230 Avenue of the Americas
New York, NY 10020

Also available in an Aladdin library edition.
Designed by Sammy Yuen, Jr.
The text of this book was set in Palatino.

Printed in the United States of America
2 4 6 8 10 9 7 5 3 1
Library of Congress Control Number 2004102671
ISBN 0-689-86035-8

For Kathleen Clark,
with love and gratitude

TABLE OF CONTENTS

Book Three of

THE
KLONDIKE
KID

Trilogy

Adventure in Gold Town

CHAPTER ONE

❧ Waiting for the Ice ❧

When I opened my eyes, it was just getting light.

"Today," I whispered, scrambling out of my sleeping bag. "It just has to happen today!"

I grabbed my boots, being careful not to wake Erik. It wasn't easy to get to the edge of the lake. I had to zigzag in and out through a maze of tents. Thousands of people were crowded here by Lake Bennett, all waiting for the same thing.

And I wanted to be the first to see it.

At last I reached the shore. Snowcapped mountains rose on either side of the long, narrow lake. As I scanned the surface, my heart fell. The water was still clogged with thick, slushy ice.

"Come on, sun!" I grumbled out loud. "Come out and melt this ice."

Suddenly a heavy hand came down on my shoulder. Startled, I whirled around.

A tall, burly man loomed over me. With his dark, dirt-covered clothes and bushy beard, he looked like a giant brown bear. The man reached over and ruffled my hair.

"Hey, Klondike Kid, you're up early again." His voice was gruff, but Big Al's warm brown eyes twinkled.

"It's taking forever for the ice to go out," I cried. "I was so sure there'd be a path of open water this morning."

The ice had been breaking up for weeks. Every day it groaned and crackled, the sounds splitting the air like sharp cracks of thunder. Added to that were the noises of boat-building—crashing trees, pounding hammers, and whining saws. The tent city at Lake Bennett was a noisy place.

Like Erik Larsen, Big Al, and me, everyone here had made the long journey over the mountains, hauling load after load of gear. For weeks, folks had been working feverishly to build boats. Everybody had the same plan: to make the trip down the Yukon River to Dawson City—and the promise of gold.

More than a year before, gold had been discovered on Rabbit Creek, a tributary of the Klondike River. From Erik's map, I knew Dawson sat on the Klondike where it enters the Yukon River. It was growing into a real boomtown, Big Al said.

"I don't understand why the ice is still here. It's almost the end of May," I complained to Big Al, digging my hands into my pockets. "Yesterday I spotted a grouse with chicks. And I can see a patch of purple wildflowers on that slope."

"It'll happen any day now, kid," Big Al assured me, running his thick fingers through his beard, trying to comb out the tangles. "Then there'll be a rush like you won't believe. Why, I reckon there's probably twenty thousand folks here, and maybe seven thousand boats."

He paused and looked me straight in the eye. "Davey, I know you're eager to get to Dawson to keep looking for your uncle Walt. But I don't aim to head out right away. We'll wait a few days and let others get ahead."

"Why?" I asked. My words tumbled out. "If you're worried about Erik, he's fine now. He's gotten stronger every day."

I was glad Erik felt better. I owed him a lot. The young photographer I'd met months ago in Seattle hadn't wanted an eleven-year-old orphan tagging along to the Klondike. He could have turned me in when he discovered I'd stowed away on the same steamship. Or he could have left me in Skagway,

4

Alaska, with my friend Hannah Clark and her family.

Instead, Erik and I had become a team. I helped him sell his photographs to the gold seekers. And we'd hauled all our food and supplies over the Chilkoot Trail into Canada, despite bad storms, the steep trail, and Erik getting sick.

"It's not about Erik, Davey," Big Al told me. "You're right, he's stronger now, and for a 'cheechako,' he does pretty well. All Erik cares about is his pictures, so he doesn't let gold fever cloud his wits like some of these fools."

Big Al was a "sourdough," an old-timer, and he didn't think much of the thousands of "cheechakos," the name the Indians gave to newcomers.

Big Al put his hand on my shoulder. "We have to wait. Trust me on this, Davey. You and I have come a long way together too. I don't aim to lose you now."

Big Al and I *had* come a long way from Mrs. Tinker's Seattle boarding house, when I'd suspected him of stealing my savings. I'd been frightened of him for a long time. But when Erik got sick on Chilkoot Pass, Big Al had been there to help us.

"I don't understand," I persisted, frowning. "Why can't we go as soon as the ice is out? You've built us a good, strong boat. And you've been down the Yukon River before."

"It's not me I'm worried about. It's these other cheechakos," replied Big Al, pointing toward the sea of white tents. "Have you seen the boats they've built? Some aren't more than log rafts! Dawson is nearly two thousand miles away. We can get there on the river, but the rapids are dangerous. I won't take a chance of running into the wrecks of other boats."

"Wrecks?" I repeated.

Big Al nodded grimly. "They don't know

6

it yet, but some of these Klondike stamped-ers are gonna die on these waters."

No matter how much I argued, Big Al wouldn't budge. I knew he was probably right. Still, I wanted to get to Dawson so badly I could hardly stand it.

Momma had died more than a year ago. Ever since, I'd been trying to find my uncle, the only family I had. In his last letter, Uncle Walt had said he was in the far north seeking his fortune. That's why I felt sure he was in Dawson, near the gold. But this waiting made me feel as if I was stuck in a bad dream. Sometimes I wondered if I'd ever get there.

A few mornings later, I felt so down-hearted I decided to make breakfast before checking the ice. I got busy mixing up batter for sourdough pancakes. When Erik stumbled out of the tent, I poured him a cup of strong, black tea.

"Thanks, Davey," he said with a grin.

"You sure learned a lot from Cook back in Mrs. Tinker's boarding house."

Cook, I knew, would be proud of me. Just last week I'd sent her a letter from the tent post office at Lake Bennett, telling her how an old-timer had given me some sourdough starter.

"Keep it warm and take good care of it, kid," the man had said, spooning a soggy, bubbling mush into the can I held. "After you use some starter, just add more flour and warm water to what you have left. That way you'll never run out. The old feller who gave this starter to me got it goin' back in '49, during the California gold rush. This starter will make the best sourdough bread, biscuits, and pancakes in the North!"

Since I liked to draw, I'd also sent Cook a sketch of myself sitting outside our tent and flipping pancakes. I'd signed it, *Davey Hill, age 11 and three-quarters, youngest cook at Lake Bennett, Canada.*

Even Big Al approved of my cooking. When he ambled up, I handed him a plate piled high with golden brown pancakes.

"Now this is the real gold of the Klondike," Big Al said, settling down on a crate of Erik's photography equipment.

Between bites he said, "So, Davey, do you still feel brave enough to shoot Miles Canyon and White Horse Rapids?"

"If we ever get out of here," I said gloomily. "It's not the river that worries me. Nothing could be as hard as waiting for the ice."

"Ice? What ice?" Big Al asked.

I looked up, startled. What was he talking about?

"I just came from the lake. The ice is out," Big Al said, a broad grin lighting his face. "And in about five minutes, as soon as someone else notices it, this tent city is gonna explode into action. By sundown there'll be a thousand boats in the water. And we won't be far behind."

"Hurrah!" I yelled, flipping a pancake high in the air. "Klondike, here we come!"

CHAPTER TWO

～ Keep a Sharp ～ Lookout!

ig Al was right. Within minutes the cry went up. "The ice is out! The ice is out!"

"Are you sure we have to wait?" Erik asked Big Al as we stood on the shore and watched the first stampeders set out. "I'd love to take photographs of all these boats shooting the rapids."

Big Al shook his head. "Take my word for it. When we head down the rapids, we don't want to be in this crowd."

At that moment a woman standing nearby shouted, "Oh, help. My horse!"

I looked where she was pointing. Her raft

had broken loose while it was being loaded. Now it was drifting across the lake with one scared horse teetering in the middle.

"I hope he doesn't panic and jump in," I cried. "He looks like Dandy, Mrs. Mac's horse."

Every time I saw packhorses, I looked for Dandy. Mrs. Mac, my neighbor in Seattle, had sold Dandy to a man buying packhorses for the Klondike. Dandy was more like a big dog than a horse. Mrs. Mac had gotten tired of him trampling her flowerbeds and even getting into the house. Once she found out what the Klondike was like, she had tried to buy Dandy back, but it was too late.

"Look, they've got him," cried Erik. As we watched, some men in a nearby boat got close enough to grab hold of a rope on the raft. Soon they'd pulled the horse to shore.

"They saved one horse," Big Al grumbled, shaking his head, "but this gold fever has killed hundreds on White Pass Trail."

I nodded. I knew folks had started calling White Pass the "dead horse trail." I also knew I'd probably never see Dandy again. Or Joe, the old black dog my landlady in Seattle had sold to a man buying dogs to pull sleds.

No, both Joe and Dandy were probably dead now, like some of the stampeders themselves. Gold makes folks crazy, Big Al liked to say. Crazy enough to sell their pets, leave their families behind, and plunge into the wilderness.

And crazy enough to set out on a wild river they knew nothing about.

We launched our boat on Friday morning, June 3, 1898. About eighteen feet long, it was made of unpainted spruce. Erik and I had spent hours helping Big Al caulk the seams with pitch to make it watertight. We'd also made a sail from canvas sacks.

Big Al sat in the back, using a rudder to steer. We'd also made oars, including two

15

long ones. Big Al called the long ones "sweep oars" and said they'd come in handy on the rapids.

As we pushed off, I looked back at what was left of the tent city. It had been a lively place, almost like a real town. There was a "main street" with saloons, bakeries, eating places, and hotels, all in tents.

Now, though, it was more than half empty. Large gaps scarred the hillsides where trees had been cut down. Lake Bennett would never be a real, permanent town. It was just a stopping place on the way to gold.

"The Yukon flows north to Dawson City. Right now we're in the headwaters, where the river begins," Big Al explained. "We'll go the length of Lake Bennett, about twenty-six miles, until we come to Tagish Lake and Marsh Lake. At Tagish, we cross Windy Arm."

"What's Windy Arm?" I wanted to know.

"It's a tricky place, almost like a funnel. At times the winds sweep down from the peaks and whip the lake into waves high enough to sink a boat."

"Let's hope our luck holds at Windy Arm," said Erik, eyeing his crate of photography equipment on the boat. "I couldn't bear to lose my camera."

On the first night we camped on the shore of Lake Bennett, making a smoky fire to fight the swarms of mosquitoes that seemed to grow thicker every day. Bold, squawking birds called camp robbers eyed me from branches overhead, then flitted down to pick up crumbs.

The next afternoon, we crossed Windy Arm. I was nervous at first. But we were lucky. The winds were steady but not too strong, and Big Al got us through easily.

"So far, so good," I called back to Big Al.

Next thing I knew, Miles Canyon loomed ahead.

● ● ●

"Miles Canyon is one of the most dangerous spots on the Yukon," Big Al had warned.

As the steep black walls of the canyon came into view, Big Al veered toward the right shore. We found a spot to pull up the boat, then joined other stampeders on the ridge top.

Erik wandered off with his camera, while Big Al greeted an old friend, a short, stout man smoking a pipe.

"More than a hundred boats have been lost already," I heard the man say. "At least ten folks have drowned."

I stepped to the edge of the cliff and looked down. Far below, white water rushed through the narrow black walls of the canyon.

All at once I felt dizzy. My head seemed too light for my body. I swayed.

"Jumpin' Jupiter!" yelled Big Al, hauling me back. "What are you doin', Davey? Get away from the cliff!"

"Who's this?" asked the short man.

"Aw, somehow I got saddled with a kid, along with a cheechako photographer," Big Al mumbled, keeping his hand on the collar of my shirt.

The man raised his eyebrows. "You're not thinking of shooting the rapids with those two, are you, Al?"

Big Al nodded grimly. "I don't have much choice."

For nearly an hour, Big Al made Erik and me watch other boats go through Miles Canyon while he explained what was about to happen. By the time we headed back to our boat, my heart was beating fast.

"Do exactly as I say," Big Al ordered. "And remember, keep the boat away from the canyon walls."

I nodded, swallowing hard. I glanced at Erik. He looked paler than usual.

"And one more thing, Davey," hollered Big Al as we pushed off from shore. "No matter how scared you get, don't shut your eyes. Keep a sharp lookout!"

As it cut through the narrow canyon, the Yukon River churned and surged. Almost at once, I could feel the swift current grab the boat.

And then we were shooting straight ahead, toward an opening in the rocks.

"The middle!" Big Al called out. "Keep to the middle."

"The current's too strong," I yelled back, but the wind swallowed my words.

Suddenly the boat swung around sharply. Big Al had lost control. I whipped around to look for just a second.

"Watch out," Erik shouted. "Davey, watch out!"

I faced forward again. I squinted, trying to see through the foaming spray. Then my heart stopped.

A rock. Right there, sticking up out of the river. Up close, it seemed gigantic—a sharp, jagged, deadly rock. And we were headed right for it.

CHAPTER THREE

~ White Horse Rapids ~

I froze. All I could hear was churning white water. All I could see was the giant dark rock.

"Davey, your oar! Use your oar to push away from the rock," Big Al shouted. "Now!"

I went into action then. With all my might, I thrust the oar forward against the boulder. At the same moment, Big Al swung the boat back into position, heading straight through the swift channel.

And then the rock was behind us. It had all happened in seconds.

Before I could catch my breath, I heard

Erik holler, "Look out to the right. Another big rock to the right!"

"That rock's called Boat-Buster, but it won't get us," Big Al cried, sweeping past it.

All at once, the river seemed to get quiet. It widened out and slowed down. We were out of the canyon. We made for the right shore and pulled the boat up on the bank. My knees felt shaky.

"Davey, you're soaked and shivering," said Erik, wiping his own dripping face.

"I . . . I'm fine," I sputtered, sinking down on the ground and trying to catch my breath. My heart was still pounding.

We sat in silence for a few minutes. Finally I said, "Thanks, Big Al."

Big Al grinned. "One down, one to go. Three miles from here is White Horse Rapids. It's a long stretch of fast white water. Some folks say it's even more dangerous than this canyon. You about ready?"

Erik nodded grimly. I gulped.

"Sure," I croaked. "Let's go."

A little later, we came around a bend of the river.

"Meet White Horse Rapids, my friends. Get ready for some ride," Big Al boomed.

We plunged into a swirling soup of white water. Our boat bounced and slapped against the waves with terrible cracking sounds. Every minute I thought it would break apart.

Big Al kept us shooting ahead, away from hidden rocks. I was drenched with icy spray. But I kept my eyes open and my oar ready.

Then I spotted trouble. "Watch out, Big Al. A boat!"

Just ahead of us, a flat-bottomed scow had struck a rock. It lurched from side to side, out of control. It was swamped with water. Two men in the boat were yelling for help, struggling madly to get to shore before they lost everything.

Just what Big Al was afraid of—a wreck! I

thought. I shot a quick look behind me. Big Al was working the sweep oar, trying to steer us away from the boat.

Suddenly I heard a sharp crack. Big Al's long sweep oar had snapped in two.

He tried to reach for the spare oar, but it had slid just out of his reach. I was closest. Quickly, I dove for it, then pushed it toward Big Al. He caught it up in one swift motion. Turning back, I lost my balance.

"Hold on, Davey," yelled Erik, reaching out to grab me.

I was in position in a second. I wanted to be ready to use my oar to keep us away from the other boat.

We surged ahead, the river under us galloping like a mighty stampede. We were coming closer and closer to the other boat. I tried to shout, but nothing came out.

We missed it by inches, veering so close I could see the terrified faces of the men. They hollered something, but the roar of the water drowned their words. All I could do was hope they reached shore before their boat sank.

Ten minutes more, and the river seemed to toss us out of the white water. Big Al made for shore. I took a deep breath and tried to keep my teeth from chattering. Around us, I spotted a dozen or more boats, broken against rocks, some splintered in two.

Now I understood how easily boats could get wrecked on this river. It had happened to those men back there. It had almost happened to us.

"You got us through again, Al," said Erik gratefully.

"Aw, that wasn't so bad. Congratulations," Big Al replied, crinkling the corners of his eyes. "You've survived your first northern winter, and now you've beat the worst the Yukon can dish up. I'd say you're well on your way to being sourdoughs."

For the first time in weeks, I laughed.

• • •

"We're making good time now," Big Al remarked one morning more than a week later. Miles Canyon and White Horse Rapids *had* been the worst. Since then, we'd spent our days skimming along the Yukon, camping each night on shore.

"We should be in Dawson in a few days," Big Al added. "What then?"

"I'm going to find Lars Heller," Erik said. "I'm sure he's already set up his photography studio. Back in Skagway, he offered me a job, and I hope he can still use me. How about you, Al?"

"Guess I'll head out to the creeks around the Klondike River to check on some old pals and see if they've had any luck. I bet the best claims have already been staked by others, though," he said.

Big Al laughed and went on, "With my luck, I'll probably end up making ends meet by sweeping gold dust off the saloon floors. And I won't be the only one."

Big Al turned to me. "What about you, Klondike Kid?"

"I'll earn my keep helping Erik with his photographs, I guess."

"That's not all," Erik said, putting his hand on my arm.

"No," I admitted. "Every chance I get I'm going to look for Uncle Walt."

I tried to sound sure of myself. I even smiled. But inside, I suddenly felt just as scared as I had on the rapids of the Yukon.

Big Al and Erik had their own plans—their own lives. I couldn't expect them to look after me forever. What if I didn't find Uncle Walt in Dawson? What would I do then?

CHAPTER FOUR

~ Trouble in ~ Dawson City

We arrived in Dawson City on Monday, June 20, at exactly three in the afternoon. It was five days after my birthday. I was twelve years old, and I had made it to the Klondike at last.

"I can hardly believe we're here," I said.

Erik was excited too. "Just think, it's been almost a year since we heard about the gold."

The waterfront was jammed with boats, three and four deep. We couldn't get close to shore, so we tied our boat to another one. Then we had to climb in and out of boats to unload our gear. Erik and I found a spot not far away to pitch our tent.

Big Al cleared his throat. "Well, I guess this is good-bye for a while."

"But . . . Big Al, are you coming back?" I asked.

Big Al grabbed me in a quick bear hug. "Don't you worry, Klondike Kid. I'll be back."

Erik and I watched Big Al lumber off.

"You know something, Davey? I think I'm going to miss him," said Erik after a minute. "But we should be fine here without Al's help. After all, what can happen to us in Dawson?"

I swallowed hard. I couldn't help wondering if I'd ever see Big Al again.

We trudged through the deep mud of Front Street, keeping an eye out for Lars Heller's photography studio. Many of the town's businesses were still in tents. But wooden buildings were taking shape before our eyes.

We had to climb over piles of lumber. The clatter of hammers filled the air.

On the corner of Front Street and Princess Street, we saw a handsome, three-story hotel being built. We stopped to watch.

"Looks like this will be pretty fancy," remarked Erik.

"You better believe it! A sharp business-woman named Belinda Mulrooney is having it built," said a workman nearby. "The Fairview Hotel should be open by the end of July. If you strike it rich, you can afford to eat oysters in the dining room, cooked by a real chef!"

"Oysters!" I repeated in astonishment as we walked on. "It seems like Dawson has almost everything Seattle does. I've already seen a bank, a newspaper office, hotels, restaurants, and hardware stores."

"Don't forget the saloons and dance halls. I bet this town never sleeps," Erik remarked. "We're so far north it's light almost all the time now that summer's here."

"Look, Erik. There's Lars Heller's studio." I read the sign on a small frame building. "'Scenic Views. Send Your Photographs Home to Loved Ones!'"

We stopped to look at the pictures on display. "Erik, here's one of Miles Canyon," I said. "I'd like to buy it to send to Hannah. She won't believe I went down it in a boat."

"Davey, I think I'll head inside to talk to Lars Heller," said Erik. "I'll see you at the tent later."

Erik disappeared inside.

And then I was alone in the Klondike, where I'd dreamed of being for so long. For a few minutes I stood still as people streamed past me. Some were miners and stampeders, just off the trail. But I also saw ladies and gentlemen looked like prosperous business owners.

I'd never dreamed Dawson would be this crowded. How would I be able to find Uncle Walt? I hadn't seen him in such a long time.

I wasn't even sure I remembered what he looked like.

All I can do is ask, I told myself. *Ask and hope.* Then, squaring my shoulders, I walked up to the first hotel I saw, opened the door, and went in.

"Did you have any luck?" Erik wanted to know at supper as I spooned some beans onto his tin plate.

I shook my head. I'd gone up and down Front Street, asking every saloon keeper, clerk, and store owner I saw, "Do you know a young fellow by the name of Walt Thomas?"

Most had simply shrugged. One man told me, "This town has grown to thirty thousand folks overnight, with more pouring in every hour."

Erik put his hand on my arm. "Don't give up, Davey. Just be patient and keep your eyes open."

• • •

Soon we settled into a routine. Some days Erik stayed in town taking pictures of Dawson. Other times he walked along the creeks. He photographed miners as they dug thirty or forty feet into the ground, then used water to rinse the dirt and gravel and separate out the gold. To do this, some miners had built large, complicated wooden systems on the bare hillsides.

Just as I'd done in Skagway, I helped deliver photographs to the miners. I also cooked our meals. And that's where I ran into trouble. Oh, I still liked to cook. And we could buy almost anything we needed in Dawson.

My big problem was the dogs.

Dogs. Big dogs and medium-size dogs. Black, white, and brown dogs. Mean dogs and shy dogs. Sad, downhearted-looking dogs, and happy-go-lucky, grinning dogs. All of them hungry, and all of them causing trouble in Dawson City.

Dawson was full of stray dogs. Most were sled dogs. Their owners had used them to haul supplies over the snow in the winter. But now the snow was gone. The owners were gone too. Some were out digging for gold. Others had given up and gone home.

Either way, it meant the same thing: hungry, abandoned dogs left to fend for themselves. The dogs roamed around in packs. They ran through the streets, bothering people. At night they howled. They got into fights, snarling and battling over scraps of food.

Whenever we left the tent, I had to make sure all our food containers were closed up tightly. And as soon as the smells of cooking drifted into the air, it wasn't long before a pack of dogs came sniffing around.

"Get away!" I yelled one night, banging my wooden spoon against a pot. Six scrawny dogs slowly moved off.

"Everyone talks about what a nuisance they are," said Erik. "But no one does anything."

As I was cleaning up after breakfast the next morning, a thin black dog stayed behind after the rest of his pack drifted away. He didn't try to come close. He just settled himself a short distance away, watching me with enormous brown eyes.

I looked at him. Suddenly my heart beat fast.

"Joe?" I asked. The dog wagged his tail weakly and whined.

Could it really be Joe?

CHAPTER FIVE

~Sourdough Pancakes~

"Is that you, Joe?" I asked again.

I held my breath. But then my heart sank. It wasn't my old friend. This dog looked a lot like Joe, but he was young, not much more than a puppy. He must have been beautiful once. Now his dull, matted coat barely hid his ribs. One ear was tattered and scarred.

"I wonder if you were someone's pet, stolen out of your own yard in Seattle," I said in a soft voice. "Or maybe someone sold you, just like Mrs. Tinker sold old Joe."

The dog yelped and thumped his tail against the ground. He wiggled a little

39

closer, his eyes fixed on the pancake.

Kneeling down, I held it out to him. "Here, boy."

The dog looked at me. Then he snatched it and swallowed the pancake in one gulp. He sat up straight in front of me, barked twice—and grinned.

He seemed friendly, so I carefully reached out and patted his head. "Joe Two. That's what I'll call you. You're not wild at all, are you? I bet you *were* somebody's pet."

At that moment two stampeders came up. "Hey, kid, those sourdough pancakes you cook up every morning smell delicious. Would you be willing to sell us some? We'll pay you double the going rate."

"They're all gone today," I said. Suddenly I was struck by an idea. "But look for me tomorrow, and you can get a stack for fifty cents."

After they were gone, I turned to face my new dog.

"Joe Two," I said solemnly. "You and these

other dogs don't deserve what happened to you. But I think I know a way to help."

"A what?" asked Erik when I told him my plan.

"A dog pound! I want to start a dog pound," I repeated. "Erik, do you remember that dog hospital we saw in Dyea last winter? Well, Dawson needs something like that—a shelter for all these stray dogs the miners don't want in the summer."

"Davey, in Dyea people were willing to pay for their dogs to be cared for because they needed them on the trail," Erik replied. "But the miners here don't need dogs in the summer. And they don't want to take care of them."

Erik eyed Joe Two uncertainly. "We might be able to afford to keep this one, if you really want. But there are dozens of dogs roaming Dawson. How are you planning to buy enough food to feed them all? And where will you put them?"

"Don't worry, Erik," I assured him. "I've got a plan."

By the next afternoon I was ready. I loaded up my backpack, then Joe Two and I started at one end of Front Street.

"I think you should wait outside," I told him. Joe Two grinned up at me and cocked his head. "Oh, all right. Come on."

Squaring my shoulders, I opened the door of the saloon and we walked in. Several men stood at the bar, while a few others sat at small tables scattered around the room.

"Hey, weren't you here just the other day looking for somebody?" asked the bartender.

I nodded. "Yes, sir. I'm trying to find my uncle. But until then, there's something I have to do. I . . . I wonder, can I post a sign in your window?"

"What's it say?" the bartender wanted to know.

Opening my backpack, I took out one of my signs. At the top was a drawing I'd made of a sad-eyed dog. Joe Two had been a good model. In a slow, clear voice I read:

DAVEY'S SOURDOUGH PANCAKE STAND

FRONT STREET, 7–9 A.M. DAILY

ALL PROCEEDS TO BENEFIT THE

MARY ELLEN HILL MEMORIAL DOG SHELTER

HELP STRAY DOGS! KEEP DAWSON'S STREETS SAFE!

PROPRIETOR, DAVID HILL, AGE 12

I looked around. Everyone in the room had stopped talking. All the men stared at me as if they expected me to say something else. I shifted from one foot to the other.

"Mary Ellen Hill was my mother," I explained. "After she died, I lived in Mrs. Tinker's boarding house in Seattle. I had a friend there; a dog called Joe. But she sold him to be a sled dog."

I pointed. "This here is Joe Two. I just

adopted him. But there are lots of other dogs in Dawson that need help."

The bartender cleared his throat. "Where are you planning on putting this dog shelter, kid?"

"I . . . I'm not sure yet," I said. "If I can raise enough money, I'll buy some fencing, and find a spot on the outskirts of town near the river so I can give the dogs water and baths, too."

I paused, trying to think what else to tell them. All I could think of was, "I make really good sourdough pancakes."

At that, the bartender threw back his head and laughed. I felt my face get hot. *This was a stupid idea*, I thought. *I might as well leave right now.*

The bartender turned to the room. "Well, boys, what do you think of this kid's plan? Can we help Dawson Dave?"

To my surprise, they began to clap and cheer.

CHAPTER SIX

∽ The Mary Ellen Hill ∽ Memorial Dog Shelter

"You won't believe it, Erik," I said that evening outside our tent. "One man in the saloon offered to let me use a stable he owns. It has a yard with a fence strong enough to keep dogs in. Two other fellows said they'd help round up dogs with their horse and cart."

"All this in one day?" Erik asked, sipping his coffee.

"That's not all," I went on, so excited I almost forgot to stir the beans. "A grocery store owner says I can set up my stand outside

46

his door. He even promised to donate some flour for the pancakes."

"Well, it looks like you've got your work cut out for you," observed Erik.

"I'd better make a list right now. That's what Cook always did before she sent me to the market," I said, dishing out beans onto our tin plates. But instead of eating, I pulled out my pencil and sketchbook. "Let's see. I'll need to get some old containers for food and water."

"You'll also need volunteers," Erik suggested between bites. "You can't take care of all those dogs alone. Maybe you could put an ad in the *Klondike Nugget* announcing the shelter."

I added that to my list. "That's a good idea. I wish Hannah was here to help."

When the list was finished, I read it to Erik. He nodded in approval.

"It's good to see you happy, Davey.

You're a bright kid," said Erik. Then he added, "We should start thinking about your future."

"My future?"

"School," said Erik. "I read in the newspaper that a lady named Lulu Craig plans to open a private school here in Dawson. You could go there this winter. Or you could return to Skagway and stay with the Clarks. I'm sure Hannah would like it if you went to her school."

"Go back to Skagway?" I repeated. I didn't want to think about school, or make plans for the winter. I wasn't ready to stop looking for Uncle Walt. "Erik, you don't believe I'm ever going to find Uncle Walt, do you?"

"I don't know, Davey," said Erik softly. "But you can't look forever."

He reached over and put his hand on my arm. "I just want to help you do what's best."

"Don't worry about me. Uncle Walt is

bound to show up any day now," I said firmly, closing my sketchbook and getting to my feet. "Once he sees the name of the dog shelter, he'll know I'm here."

Erik looked puzzled. "How?"

"Because he'll see the signs I made for the dog shelter. He'll know Mary Ellen Hill was Momma's name when she was married. And then he'll find me. I'm sure of it."

"I hope so, Davey," said Erik. "I hope so."

"Come on, Joe Two," I whispered the next morning when I climbed out of the tent. "It's our first day at Davey's Sourdough Pancake Stand. We want everything to go well."

As it turned out, I had nothing to worry about. By eight the batter was gone. I sold every sourdough pancake that I made. Best of all, I got lots of donations for the Mary Ellen Hill Memorial Dog Shelter.

"You're welcome to come back tomorrow, Davey," said the grocery store man when I went inside to thank him. "Oh, and my wife says she's got some old containers you can use as dog bowls."

Pancakes and dogs. Dogs and pancakes. From that day on I didn't have time to think about much else. I didn't worry about school, what would happen in the winter, or what Big Al was up to. I hardly even had time to worry about Uncle Walt. Because for now I had a mission—and a job to do.

Usually I mixed up a big batch of sourdough pancake batter in a large, clean bucket at night before going to sleep. Early each morning, I hauled my supplies and camp stove over to Front Street.

The pancake stand was such a success I usually sold out early. Then I'd pack up, wash my stack of tin plates and forks, and head over to the Mary Ellen Hill Memorial Dog Shelter. We began with twenty dogs, but by the end of August there were nearly fifty.

I bought a big logbook. I wrote down all the money I got, and all my expenses. I also kept track of the dogs. That was Hannah Clark's idea. I'd written to tell her about the shelter, and I'd gotten a letter back.

"Dear Davey, we are all fine here in Skagway. It's wonderful that you are helping dogs. My daddy keeps track of all his horses, so I think you should do the same," Hannah wrote. "If people come to get a dog, write down their names, too. That way you can make them be responsible."

So I gave each dog a name, a number, and a description. I wrote down the date it came to the shelter. I left a space for an owner, too.

"You're the number one dog," I told Joe Two. Under the column for owner, I wrote my own name.

"I hope Big Al comes back soon," I told Joe Two one sunny morning after I'd finished filling all the water containers for the dogs. "I

think he'd be proud of this shelter."

Just then I saw a man walking slowly toward the shelter. I squinted. Did I know him? My heart gave a little leap. But as he got closer, I knew he wasn't Uncle Walt.

The miner was weighted down with a large pack, an axe, and a shovel. "Someone said you have dogs here. I'm here to pick up mine."

"What does he look like?" I asked.

The man let his eye wander over the dogs. "There he is," he said, pointing to a spot behind me. "It's that one."

I turned. He was pointing at Joe Two.

CHAPTER SEVEN

～ Joe Two ～

Behind me, Joe Two was stretched out in the sunshine, fast asleep.

"Yup, that's him," repeated the man. "I recognize the scar on his ear. Goes by the name of Nugget."

"You can't have that dog," I blurted.

The man took a step closer. His voice rose. "I tell you, kid. That's my dog. I paid good money for him."

The man was angry. I could feel my own anger rising, surging like the Yukon. I wanted to shout, *You abandoned this dog, and you can't have him back. He's mine now!*

I thought fast. I had to find a way to trick this miner out of wanting Joe Two. But how?

"Well, um . . . it's not that I don't *want* to give you this dog, sir. I'd be glad if you took him off my hands," I began slowly, forcing myself to smile. "But I can tell you're sharp. I bet no one puts anything over on you."

The man puffed up a little at being praised. "I'm no fool, that's for sure."

"Just as I thought. Because the truth is, although this dog might have been worth something when you had him, he's almost worthless now." I shook my head sadly. "He's got a disease."

"A disease? He don't look that bad to me."

I leaned in close and whispered, "I suspect his insides are being eaten up by Klondike worms."

"Klondike worms!" The man made a face and took a step back. "Never heard of such a thing."

"You haven't? Why, these worms are as nasty as Klondike mosquitoes, let me tell you. I've got him separated from the other dogs, so he won't make them sick," I went on. "But I don't think he'll last till Christmas."

"Well, I don't want a sick dog," the man said, wrinkling his nose in disgust.

"It just so happens I had a dog come in the other day that might suit a sharp miner like yourself." I pointed to a large brown dog. "He's big and strong. Fast, too. So fast we call him Streak."

Fifteen minutes later, the man left with Streak. Joe Two woke up and stood beside me as we watched them go. Joe Two whined a little.

"Don't worry," I told him, scratching behind his ear. "I named that dog Streak because he's always running away. If that miner's a bit mean, Streak will be gone in a flash. The man will end up carrying his own gear. And it serves him right."

Joe Two barked in agreement.

Before I knew it, the short northern summer was over. By October, the darkness began to settle in. Every morning frost lay thickly on the ground. Chunks of ice clogged the Klondike River, and some of the smaller creeks were already frozen. Each night, the muddy streets of Dawson froze into ruts.

Erik still wanted me to go to school, but I was too busy. Now that more snow was falling, miners were coming to the Mary Ellen Hill Memorial Dog Shelter every day. They wanted their dogs back so they could use them to pull sleds.

"Good morning, gentlemen," I'd say when they appeared. "I need your names and the names of your dogs for my logbook here. And we'd sure appreciate a donation for the Mary Ellen Hill Memorial Dog Shelter."

The men usually pulled out little sacks of gold dust and sprinkled some onto the little scale I'd bought. I also made each miner sign a paper saying he wouldn't abandon his dogs again.

"Now, if you don't want your dogs next summer, bring them here," I told the miners. "We'll charge you ten dollars a month to buy bacon to feed them. But they'll be in better shape when you need them next fall."

Then one morning, just after some miners had left with their dogs, Joe Two began to bark. Before long, the rest of the dogs in the Mary Ellen Hill Memorial Dog Shelter were howling along with him.

I looked around. At first I didn't notice anything unusual. Then I saw it. A thick curl of black smoke was rising up over town.

"Fire! Dawson's on fire," I said aloud.

Suddenly I remembered. Erik was at the photography studio. Pictures! The studio

was full of camera equipment, glass plate negatives, and photographs. If the studio burned, all the wonderful pictures Erik and Lars Heller had taken of the Klondike would be lost.

"Come on, Joe Two," I yelled, already beginning to run. "We've got to help Erik."

CHAPTER EIGHT

~ Fire in Gold Town ~

"The post office is gone," I heard a man yell. "The Greentree Hotel is in flames."

The muddy streets were filled with men and women, shouting and running this way and that. I stopped for a minute, panting, to catch my breath.

"Where did it start?" I asked a man standing near me.

"In a saloon," he said. "It's racing through the business district."

Another man ran up with two axes and handed one to his friend. "Let's go, Hank.

We're chopping down buildings now to keep it from spreading."

"Aren't there any hoses?" I called out after them.

"All the new firefighting equipment is sitting in the warehouse because the town hasn't raised enough money to pay for it yet!" Hank yelled over his shoulder.

"Come on, Joe Two," I called. "Stay close now."

Crowds filled the streets. The smoke was thicker now, and small particles of ash drifted through the air.

"Erik!" I shouted as we came to the studio.

Erik appeared in the doorway carrying fragile glass plates in his arms. "Davey, you shouldn't be here. It's too dangerous. We're in the path of the fire."

I looked around. Crackling red flames were already devouring the wooden buildings on the block. "I want to help." I reached out to take the glass plates from him.

Erik nodded toward some equipment already piled up in the middle of the muddy street. "Put them with the rest. They should be safe there."

"All right." I carried the load and put it down carefully. I could feel the scratch of the smoky air in my throat. "Joe Two, come stand guard next to this equipment."

The minutes passed in a blur. We raced back and forth. It got harder and harder to breathe. Near us, women and men had formed a line to the river and were passing up buckets of water. The air turned thick and gray, and I could hear the sharp crackling of the flames.

"We've got almost everything," yelled Erik's partner, Lars Heller. "Just a few more trips."

I raced back into the building and grabbed Erik's camera and tripod. As I made for the door, two men came charging in. I could barely make them out through the smoke. At first I thought it was Erik and

Lars. But one of these men was much bigger.

"Davey! Get yourself out of here, kid," a voice growled. "The fire's too close."

My mouth flew open. "Big Al!"

Before I could say another word, he pushed me out the door.

Joe Two jumped up and tried to lick my face as I staggered into the street.

"It's too dangerous to go back again," Erik said, taking the equipment from me.

"There's nothing more we can do." Lars sighed, his shoulders slumped in defeat.

Around us, men were still chopping at nearby buildings, trying to slow the fire. Lars and Erik looked exhausted, their faces and arms covered with soot. We sat in the middle of a pile of cameras, darkroom equipment, and boxes of photographs. Nearby, a grocery store owner and his wife had managed to drag out bottles, cans, and jars right off the shelves.

I grabbed Erik's arm. "Big Al! I saw Big Al. He's inside."

We peered through the smoky haze. Where was he?

"There he is. He's all right!" Erik cried at last.

Big Al appeared. He'd hooked his shoulders through two chairs, and held a table over his head.

"That's all the furniture I could carry," he announced, lowering everything to the ground.

I rushed to give him a hug. "You came back, Big Al."

"Yup, and I brought a friend." Big Al turned to look as a second man appeared out of the swirling smoke.

Lars rushed up to take a crate from the man's arms. The smoke was so thick I could barely see his face.

"Well, Davey," said Big Al, bending down to speak softly into my ear. "Ain't you gonna give your uncle Walt a hug too?"

CHAPTER NINE

❧ True Riches ❧

The Fairview Hotel had survived the fire. That night, after a visit to the bathhouse, we went to Belinda Mulrooney's famous restaurant—all five of us: Uncle Walt, Big Al, Erik, Lars Heller, and me.

At first Lars hadn't wanted to come. Losing the studio was a big blow. But Big Al had clapped him on the back and said, "Walt here and I are treating. Besides, not all was lost. You have your equipment and your precious photos. We can get that studio rebuilt in a matter of weeks."

I'd been begging to hear how Big Al had

found Uncle Walt. But every time I asked, Big Al just said, "Tonight. We'll explain everything tonight."

I was so excited I practically flew to the Fairview. Stepping onto the porch of the three-story hotel, I stopped and told Joe Two, "All right, now. You stay outside and wait."

"Nonsense, young man, it's too cold tonight," came a voice. I turned to see the Fairview's owner herself. Belinda Mulrooney was a young woman with spectacles and gold nuggets in her belt. "My own Nero, a St. Bernard, has a cozy place to sleep in the basement of the Fairview. You can leave your dog with him while you dine."

"Davey, your eyes are big as saucers," Uncle Walt said with a laugh as we walked into the dining room, his arm around my shoulders. I leaned close to him. I'd never known him well, but he reminded me of Momma somehow. Already he seemed like home.

"Wow, just look at this place," I breathed,

touching the sparkling white tablecloth. "The chandeliers sparkle like stars."

As soon as we'd ordered, I begged Big Al to begin. "I can't wait *any* longer."

Big Al laughed, his brown eyes twinkling with fun. "Well, then. I knew finding your uncle Walt in Dawson would be like looking for a needle in a haystack. There was another thing, too. If, as you said, he was already up north in 1896, then most likely he'd already be working at a claim."

Uncle Walt brushed his dark hair out of his eyes and nodded. "Al's right. I was in Alaska when I heard about the discovery of gold in August 1896. I wrote you and your mother a letter that fall, on my way to the Klondike. I know now, Davey, that you sent me a letter after your momma died, but I never got it. I wrote again last August, but by then you'd gone."

"So, you haven't been in Dawson all along?" I wanted to know.

"No," explained Uncle Walt. "My partners and I staked a claim on Bonanza Creek, near the town of Grand Forks. It's about fifteen miles away."

"But . . . but how did you find him, Big Al?"

"I took a lesson from you, Davey. I didn't give up," Big Al replied with a laugh. "From the time I left here in June, seems like I walked up and down every creek in the Yukon Territory."

I picked up my crystal water goblet. "I'd like to make a toast."

"What shall we toast to, Davey?" asked Erik.

"True riches," I declared. "Friends and family."

By the end of the meal I was so full and sleepy I could barely keep my eyes open. But there was one more question I had to ask.

"Uncle Walt, what happens now?"

Uncle Walt grinned. "Well, I've had my fill of digging deep into frozen hillsides looking for gold. I'm not rich, but I've got enough to start my own business, something I've wanted to do for a long time."

"And what business is that?" asked Erik.

"A restaurant," Uncle Walt announced. "I did a lot of the cooking up here, and it turns out I like it a lot."

A restaurant! Everyone burst into laughter.

"You two really are related," Erik said with a grin. "You like the same things."

Uncle Walt turned toward me. "So, Davey, if you're willing, I thought we'd head back to Seattle and start our own restaurant."

"On one condition," I said, trying not to laugh.

"What's that?" Uncle Walt wanted to know.

"I think my old friend Cook and I should

be in charge of cooking breakfast. I guarantee we'll make the best sourdough pancakes and biscuits in Seattle!"

By the time we were ready to leave Dawson, most of the dogs at the Mary Ellen Hill Memorial Dog Shelter had found owners. But there were enough left to form a dog sled team, so Uncle Walt and I could make the long journey over the snow to Skagway.

It was hard to say good-bye to Erik and Big Al. Erik had decided to stay in Dawson and work with Lars Heller, at least for a while.

Erik promised to find someone to operate the dog shelter next summer. "And if I can't, I'll do it myself." Then he handed me an envelope. "There's that photograph of Miles Canyon you wanted for Hannah. And some pictures for yourself, to help you remember your Klondike adventure."

"Thank you, Erik," I said, giving him a hug. "What about you, Big Al?"

"Well, first I'm helping to organize a volunteer fire department for Dawson. We need to get that firefighting equipment paid for and train some fellows to use it," said Big Al, ruffling my hair with his thick hand. "After that, maybe I'll head to Nome, Alaska. I like adventure well enough. And who knows? Seems like a likely place for gold. Might as well have a look for myself."

I hugged Big Al, too. "I'll never forget you."

Big Al pulled a white handkerchief out of his pocket. "Oh, speaking of that, Davey, I got something for you to remember me by."

Slowly I unwrapped the handkerchief. Inside were twelve small gold nuggets. My mouth dropped open. "Thanks, Big Al! Now I can give one to my friend Tag, in Seattle, just like I promised."

I looked at Big Al and Erik. "Will I see you both again?" I asked them.

"Save us the best table at the restaurant," Big Al promised.

We arrived in Skagway in time to spend Christmas with the Clarks. Hannah, her brother, Rusty, and little sister, Ellen, had all grown a lot. Hannah said Skagway felt like home now, and we had fun exploring while Uncle Walt and I waited for the next steamship to Seattle.

"I appreciate you taking our sled dogs and selling them," Uncle Walt said to Hannah's father one night at supper.

"Except for Joe Two," put in Hannah. "He's going with Davey, of course."

"I'm happy to find good homes for the dogs," said Mr. Clark. "But I have a favor to ask in return."

"What's that?" asked Uncle Walt.

"A few days ago, a fellow came by with a horse. Of all the packhorses he had on the White Pass Trail, this is the only one that lived," Mr. Clark began. "This horse never tore off a pack, and no matter how hard it got, he just kept on. He got stuck in the mud once, but they pulled him out."

Joe Two came to sit by my chair, and I patted his head while I listened.

"Well, the man gave me some money and asked me to arrange for the horse's passage back to Seattle," Mr. Clark said, getting up and taking an envelope from a shelf. "Seems he bought the horse from a fellow who told him the horse's original owner, a lady in Seattle, wanted him back. Now he feels this horse deserves to go home. He needs someone to bring the horse to Seattle and place an ad in the newspaper to find the lady."

Mr. Clark opened the envelope and drew out a piece of paper. "From what he told me, this horse is quite a character, always getting into things. More like a big dog . . ."

"A big dog?" I jumped to my feet so fast

the chair fell to the floor with a crash. "Where is the horse, Mr. Clark?"

"Out in the stable. But I have the horse's name right here," he said, a puzzled look on his face. "It's . . ."

"Dandy!" Mr. Clark and I said at the same time.

With Joe Two at our heels, Uncle Walt, the Clark family, and I clattered out to the stable. A horse stuck his nose out of his stall and looked curiously at this swarm of visitors. I recognized him right away.

"I can't believe it. It really is Dandy!" I told Uncle Walt. "We can deliver this horse right to Mrs. Mac's doorstep. Dandy lived near us in Seattle. He loved to eat flowers and was always getting into Mrs. Mac's house. I thought for sure he was dead."

"Hey, Davey, I have an idea," said Hannah, pulling on my sleeve. "Maybe you and your uncle can name your restaurant after him."

"Dandy's Restaurant," said Uncle Walt, trying it out. "Sounds fine and dandy to me."

Joe Two barked twice and grinned.

"Dandy," I said, scratching my old friend's ears. "We're all going home."

Sourdough Starter Recipe

The history of sourdough breads goes back thousands of years to the Egyptians. Moistening flour and leaving it exposed to air causes it to ferment and expand. This sourdough starter can then be used to make bread rise. Information and various recipes for making sourdough starter are available on the Internet. This is the one I used to make sourdough starter and sourdough pancakes at home.

Sourdough Starter
2 cups enriched flour
2 cups warm water
1 package dry yeast

Mix until blended in a large ceramic mixing bowl. Let stand uncovered in a warm place for 48 hours. Stir occasionally. Stir well before use. To replenish starter and keep it going, pour out the amount you need, then add 1 cup of flour and 1 cup of warm water. Let stand until it bubbles, then cover loosely and refrigerate. Use and add to your starter every two weeks.

SOURDOUGH PANCAKES

2 cups starter
1 cup flour
1/4 cup oil
1 tablespoon baking powder
1 cup milk
1 teaspoon salt
2 beaten eggs
1 teaspoon baking soda
1/4 cup sugar

Mix flour, starter, and milk, and beat until smooth. Cover loosely with wax paper and let stand in a warm place for 18 hours. Add remaining ingredients and stir until smooth. Cook in a pan or on a 400-degree griddle, using a tablespoon or so of batter for each pancake.

AUTHOR'S NOTE

"Dogs everywhere, day and night, howling, fighting, filthy, mangy dogs form one of the worst nuisances that . . . has afflicted the citizens of Dawson . . . Last year the government established a dog pound . . ."
Dawson Daily News, May 23, 1900
Quoted in *A Klondike Scrapbook*,
by Norman Bolotin

Like Davey Hill, most gold seekers who set out to reach Dawson City found that the journey took longer than expected. People first heard about the discovery of gold near the Klondike River in Canada in July 1897. Eager stampeders sailed to Skagway, Alaska, then packed their goods over the mountains to Lake Bennett or Lake Lindeman, the headwaters of the Yukon River. Many arrived after the river was frozen and were forced to wait until the spring of 1898 for the ice to melt before they could continue their journey to Dawson City.

Dawson was famous as a boomtown of

saloons, dance halls, and colorful characters (like the real Belinda Mulrooney, a successful businesswoman who makes an appearance in this book). But when I came across a newspaper story about a dog pound in Dawson, I thought that helping animals was the kind of thing Davey would want to do.

Although the main characters in *The Klondike Kid* are fictional, several real-life photographers like Erik Larsen traveled to Dawson City. One of the most famous, Eric Hegg, opened a studio in Dawson. During the fire of October 14, 1898 his studio was damaged, but the cameras, equipment, and photographs were saved. Thanks to frontier photographers like Hegg, amazing pictures of the Klondike stampede still exist.

The story of a real horse named Dandy is told in Archie Satterfield's book, *Chilkoot Pass*. He notes that a Mrs. McGuian of Seattle sold her horse named Dandy (who liked to eat flowers and to open gates) to William

Loerpabel for $30. She changed her mind, but he refused to give the horse back. Later, though, he became fond of Dandy, his only packhorse to survive White Pass Trail. The story goes that he found a man going back to Seattle and asked him to take the horse back to Mrs. McGuian.

Another Seattle woman, Florence Hartshorn, who traveled to the Klondike herself, was instrumental in establishing a memorial in 1929 to the estimated 3,000 pack animals that died on White Pass Trail. Mrs. Hartshorn's unpublished manuscripts are part of the University of Washington Special Collections, and I made use of her eyewitness accounts in writing this series.

For more about the Klondike, visit the Klondike Gold Rush Seattle Unit, National Historical Park, at *http://www.nps.gov/klse*. Another excellent resource is the University of Washington at *http://www.washington. edu/uwired/outreach/cspn/curklon/main.html*.